THE QUIET HOUSE
BY
OTTO COONTZ

LITTLE, BROWN AND COMPANY
BOSTON   TORONTO

FIRST EDITION

T 09/78

Library of Congress Cataloging in Publication Data

Coontz, Otto.
  The quiet house.

  SUMMARY: A lonely dog finds three new friends in
a surprising place.
  [1. Dogs—Fiction. 2. Friendship—Fiction]
I. Title.
PZ7.C7845Qi   [E]   78-18347
ISBN 0-316-15533-0

*Published simultaneously in Canada
by Little, Brown & Company (Canada) Limited*

PRINTED IN THE UNITED STATES OF AMERICA

For Gus and Duch

Bagsley lived alone in a very quiet house. The faucets didn't drip. The stairs never creaked. Even the clocks had no tick.

One cold and windy night, Bagsley curled up in bed with a story book. It was all about ghosts.

"This story is too scary," he said. "Now I will never get to sleep." He looked around the room wishing he had someone to talk to.

Suddenly he heard a tapping at the door. Bagsley jumped under the covers.

"It's much too late for visitors," he shivered. "If I am quiet and do not move, maybe it will go away." But the tapping grew louder. Bagsley's tail began to drum against the bedpost.

"Please, tail," he said, "we must be very still."

7

At last the tapping stopped. Bagsley tossed and turned, wondering what was at the door. He wrapped himself in a blanket and crawled out of bed. Then he tiptoed from room to room, turning on all the lights.

He crept downstairs as softly as he could. His heart was beating quickly.

"Please, heart, not so fast. I'm not in any hurry."

11

Bagsley put his ear to the door. He could not hear a sound. He opened it a crack.

"I know you're out there!" he growled in his gruffest voice. "You can't scare me!"

The wind moaned back.

13

Bagsley unlocked the door and stepped outside.

He searched everywhere.

"There is no one here," he said. "Perhaps it was only a branch tapping in the wind. How silly I was to be scared by that."

Feeling a little better, he started indoors.

15

"What's this?" he said.

There was a note tacked to his door. The note read:

Complimentary Offer! To commemorate the opening of a new shop, we are giving away free samples. One night only. Specializing in a variety of eggs for the lonely. For home delivery, call The Egg Lady at 322.

17

Bagsley read the note very carefully.

"Eggs for the lonely?" he thought. "I am a little lonely. And I didn't buy eggs today. Wouldn't an omelette be nice before bed?"

He dialed the number he found at the bottom of the note.

"Good evening," he said. "I should like to try some of your eggs."

"How many would you like?" asked The Egg Lady.

"Three would be fine, thank you," answered Bagsley.

"Three?" said the voice at the other end. "Why, you *must* be lonely."

"I will make this a party," he decided, "and make a tasty omelette. Now, whom shall I invite?"

Bagsley sat down in his most comfortable chair and opened the phone book. He started at the beginning and read right through to the end.

"Goodness," he groaned, "I don't know anyone in here!"

21

Then the doorbell rang. Bagsley
had an idea.

"I know! I will invite the delivery
boy! On such a cold night, I am
sure he would like to come sit by
my fire."

23

But when Bagsley opened the
door, he found only a basket of
eggs. There was a note attached. It
read:
    Treat gently, very fragile.

25

"No one to make an omelette for," he sighed.

He carried the basket into the kitchen.

"I guess I am not so hungry after all." Bagsley slowly climbed upstairs and crawled back into bed.

Once again, the house grew
quiet.

29

The next morning, Bagsley woke up very hungry.

"I will make French toast," he decided. "It will be light as a feather. That will cheer me up!" But when he stepped into the kitchen, he found egg shells on the floor.

"What has happened to my eggs?" he cried. A chuckle came from the basket.

"I do not think these eggs are very fresh," said Bagsley.

31

He heard a crackling sound.

"Not fresh at all!" he shouted. A furry head poked out of the basket.

"How do you do?" asked a little platypus. "My name is Gus. And that's Brenda." He pointed to a penguin walking along the counter. Brenda did not stop to say hello.

"And what is in the third egg? Or is that the one for eating?" Bagsley asked.

"Oh no, certainly not! That wouldn't do at all," replied the platypus. "That's Rose. She's an armadillo." The third egg didn't crack open. It uncurled.

"Pleased to meet you," said Rose.

"Weren't you expecting us?" Gus asked.

"Of course I was expecting you!" Bagsley answered. "Only last night I was planning a party! And now my guests have arrived!"

"We love parties!" cheered Gus.

"Oh yes!" agreed Brenda. "And I will serve the refreshments."

"Refreshments?" asked Rose. "May I have a big bowl?"

37

For the rest of the morning, they sang party songs and told their favorite jokes. Bagsley was very happy.

Later, Brenda, Gus, and Rose went outside to play badminton. Bagsley wrote each of their names in the phone book, right next to his own.

"Now," he said, "when I have a party, I will know just whom to ask."

"Hurry up, Bagsley," Rose called. "We can't start playing without you."

39